In a magical meadow
filled with rainbow
flowers lived a unicorn
named Sparkle.

Sparkle had a
shimmering pink mane, a
glittery white coat, and
a swirly horn that
changed colors.

But poor Sparkle had one tiny problem – she was the clumsiest unicorn in all the land.

Every morning, she'd trip
over her own hooves while
trying to brush her teeth
with her horn.

At breakfast, she'd accidentally dip her mane in rainbow juice instead of her cup.

When she tried to run and play with her unicorn friends, she'd stumble and roll down hills.

But Sparkle never gave up and always kept a big smile on her face.

One day, she decided to join the annual Unicorn Princess Parade.

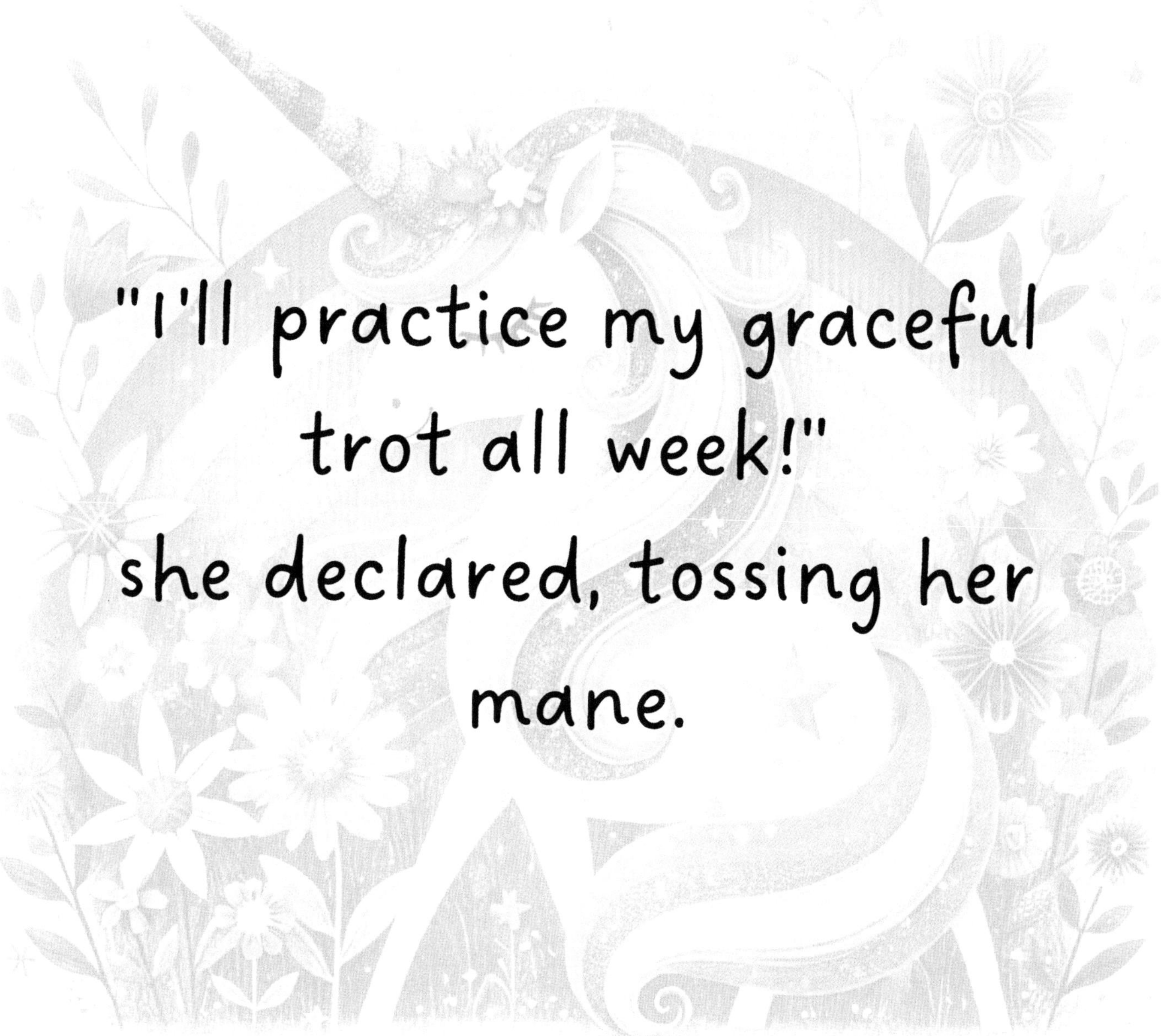

"I'll practice my graceful trot all week!" she declared, tossing her mane.

On Monday, she practiced in the garden and got tangled in flower vines.

On Tuesday, she rehearsed by the stream and fell in with a big splash!

On Wednesday, she tried in the clouds but sneezed and fell through them like rain.

On Thursday, she attempted it in the fairy forest and got fairy dust all over her horn.

On Friday, she practiced in the candy cane fields and got stuck to a giant lollipop.

On Saturday, she tried one last time in the starlight meadow and tripped over a shooting star.

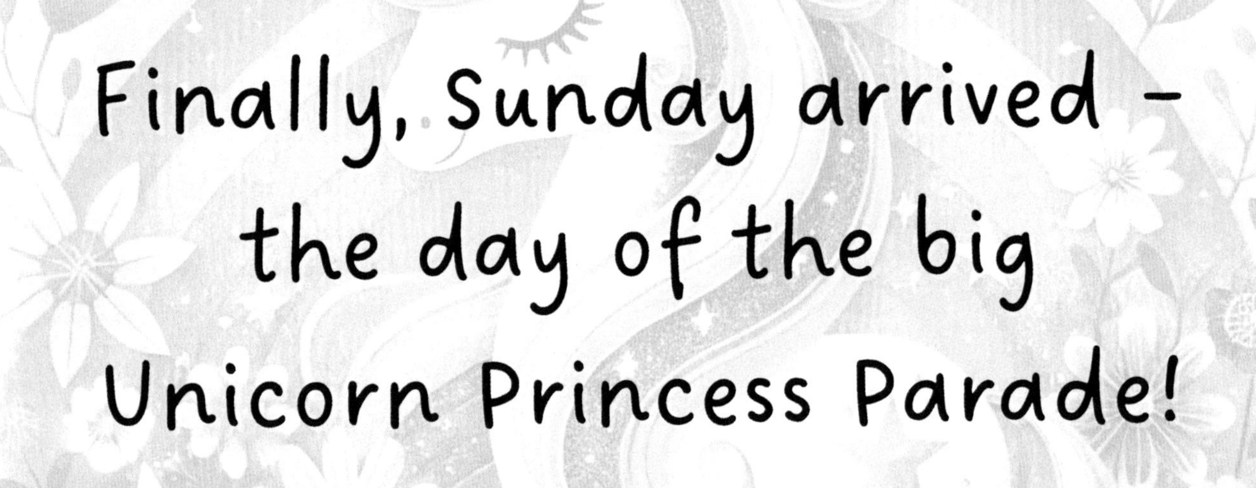

Finally, Sunday arrived - the day of the big Unicorn Princess Parade!

Sparkle lined up with all
the other unicorns,
feeling nervous but
excited.

As the parade began, Sparkle took a deep breath and started to trot.

To everyone's surprise, she didn't trip, stumble, or fall!

She pranced and
danced, her horn
sparkling with all the
colors of the rainbow.

The crowd cheered as
Sparkle passed by,
throwing glitter and
giggles.

At the end of the parade, the Unicorn Queen approached Sparkle.

"My dear,"
she said,
"you've won the award
for Most Entertaining
Unicorn!"

Sparkle was confused. "But I didn't trip or fall once!" she exclaimed.

The Queen laughed and said,
"Exactly! Your week of clumsy practice made you the best dancer of all!"

From that day on, Sparkle embraced her clumsiness and taught other unicorns how to laugh at themselves.

She became known as the happiest, most fun-loving unicorn in all the land.

And every year, she led the Unicorn Princess Parade with a skip, a trip, and a whole lot of giggles.

The End

Made in the USA
Coppell, TX
17 December 2024